Pigs! Pigs! Pigs!

Just Right Reader

Pigs!

I am Tiz, the pig!

I can go zip.

I am Pip, the pig!

I sit in a bin.

I am Riz, the pig!

Do you see my wig?

I am Fin, the pig.

I bit into a fig.

I am Sid, the pig.

Look!

A six on my bib.

Did I win?

Pigs!

We can mix up and do spins.

Fit pigs!

Pigs, pigs, pigs.

Pip, Riz, Fin, and Sid, my kin!

Phonics Fun

- Say a word.
- Tap out the sounds you hear in each word.
- Tap your shoulder for the first sound you hear.
- Tap your elbow for the second sound you hear.
- Tap your wrist for the third sound you hear.
- Say the word.

bib mix pig six

 High Frequency Words

| do | into | you |
| go | we | |

 Comprehension

Why do you think the author wrote this book?

 Decodable Words

bib	Pip
bin	Riz
bit	Sid
fig	sit
Fin	six
fit	Tiz
kin	wig
mix	win
pig	zip